Fire from Ice

by Josh Craig

illustrated by Eric Velasquez

Harcourt

Orlando   Boston   Dallas   Chicago   San Diego

Visit *The Learning Site!*

www.harcourtschool.com

The winter had been very, very cold. Little Fox did not have to exaggerate when he described the weather to his grandfather.

"It's so cold out there that a fish better not jump out of the river. The water might freeze by the time it falls back down," he said. Little Fox thought his description was a good one. He thought it was pretty accurate, too.

"Now, Little Fox," said Grandfather sternly, "be careful of what you say. You don't want to get a name like 'Tells Tall Tales,' do you?"

"Of course not, Grandfather," said Little Fox. "I want to get a name that will make you proud of me. I assure you I did not exaggerate much. It really is cold out there!"

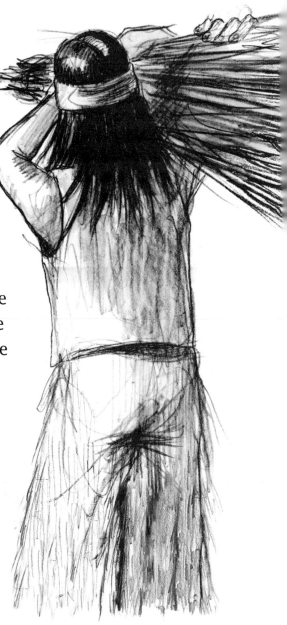

Little Fox's grandfather did not leave the warmth of his tent very often during the winter. He, like the other elders and the babies, stayed close to home most of the time. They would depend on the younger people to bring home food and wood. As long as the young people did that, the older people could keep the fires burning.

Little Fox wished he could spend more time with his grandfather. He and the other young people had much to do, though. They were getting ready for the day when they would become adults. Soon each of them would be given a new name—a name to use for the rest of his or her life. Little Fox's grandfather was the one who would give them their adult names.

This was a matter of great concern to Little Fox. Of course, he wanted his name to show that he was strong or talented in some way. Still, he was afraid he was not special enough to be given a good name.

Other boys his age could walk
through the forest with an almost
silent tread. They could do this
even though the ground might be
littered with dry sticks that would
break under the slightest pressure.
The forest floor would have to be
covered with soft moss before
Little Fox could walk silently
across it. A good name like "Silent
Tread" was out of the question for
him.

One small girl in the village was able to
stand up to anyone who bothered her. Little
Fox had noticed it one day when a group of
boys were teasing her. The girl stood up and
crossed her arms in front of herself. Then she
looked at them so sternly that they backed
down. Little Fox thought that a good name for
her might be "Stands Sternly." In fact, he had
mentioned that name to her one day, but she
didn't look very pleased at the sound of it.

The naming-day ceremony was drawing near. As soon as the snow melted, a celebration would be held. There would be feasting, games, and dancing. Then, at the end of the day, the naming ceremony would take place.

One of the games was always a bow-and-arrow contest for the boys. Each contestant would try to hit a target with an arrow from his quiver. A very skilled boy would be able to hit the mark three times before emptying his quiver. Little Fox had never hit the target even once. He would not be taking part in the bow-and-arrow contest.

One morning
Little Fox awoke
before anyone else in the
village. He had a feeling
that something was wrong.
The air just didn't feel right. It
didn't smell right, either.

He looked outside his tent and saw
the village covered by a wet, heavy
snowfall. Not only that, but all the fires had
gone out. Just before dawn, it seemed, the
person in charge of the fires had fallen asleep.

All morning the people in the village tried to start another fire, but it was impossible. Although they had wood to burn, they had no small, dry sticks to get a fire started. All their small, dry sticks had become wet in the snow. Little Fox knew this was a serious problem. If the fires weren't started soon, the people might freeze.

Just then Little Fox noticed sunlight glinting off an icicle. The heat melting the icicle reminded him of a way to start a fire. He fought to compose himself and then ran to his tent to get what he needed.

Little Fox got his quiver of arrows. Next, he felt under the corner of his sleeping blankets and pulled out a small bag. Finally, he ran to his mother to ask for some of the moss she used as a bandage for cuts.

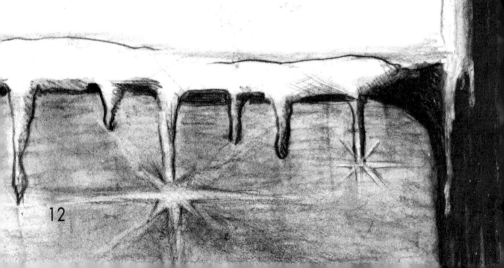

Little Fox was in luck. His mother gave him a basket full of moss. The hardest part would be finding a flat rock under all that snow. He decided to borrow one of the rocks the men used to pound tent stakes into the ground.

At last Little Fox was ready. He settled on a spot in the sun where the snow wasn't frozen and dug a hole with his flat rock. He put the rock in the hole and shook his stone collection out of the bag. Then he formed the stones into a ring on the flat rock.

Little Fox found some small wood pieces.
Then he packed them, along with some moss,
inside the ring. The ring of stones would
keep the tightly packed moss and the wood
pieces from moving.

Finally, he took an arrow, stuck one end in
the moss and sticks, and twirled the other
end between his hands for a long time.
Before long, the movement of the twirling
arrow against the sticks and moss created
enough heat to start a fire.

14

What a hero Little Fox was when his plan worked! The fire he started was used to start other fires in the village. Soon everyone was warm again.

That evening Grandfather said he had an important announcement. "Even though the naming-day ceremony is still a few days away, I have already decided on a name for Little Fox. He could not do anything more important than what he has done today. From this day forward, Little Fox will be called "Fire from Ice."

Little Fox did not want to appear too proud of his new name. He tried to compose himself, but he could not keep from smiling proudly as he heard his friends and family repeat his name. He knew now that he had something special to offer. "Fire from Ice": That sounded good.